Arnold Palmer
and the
Golfin' Dolphin

P. Byron Polakoff

Illustrated by
Deborah Mackall

Published by
Turnbull & Willoughby
1151 West Webster Avenue
Chicago, Illinois 60614

Text copyright © 1984 by P. Byron Polakoff
Pictures copyright © 1984 by Turnbull & Willoughby and P. Byron Polakoff
Manufactured in the United States of America
Cover design by Sandra Zimnicki
First Printing
10-1-84

ISBN 0-943084-14-8
ISBN 0-943084-18-0 (library binding)
5 4 3 2 1

Available at fine bookstores
everywhere or send $12.95
(plus $1.25 shipping and handling)
To: Turnbull & Willoughby
1151 West Webster
Chicago, IL 60614

For
My parents and sister, lovely wife too;
Ian, Graham and little Drew.

Special thanks to

Bill O'Conner
and
Irvin Brummell and family

The great game of golf is exciting to see;
The game's played with 14 clubs, bag, ball and tee.
To win, one must take the least number of strokes.
That sounds rather simple . . . now doesn't it, folks?

Well, don't be misled, it's a difficult game
With many fine golfers of fortune and fame
Who play for the honor of tournament gold.
Folks, now hear the tale of this tournament told.

It was a grand P.G.A. classic affair.
The world's best golfers had come to play there.
Trevino and Nicklaus and Palmer, no doubt,
And also the dolphin this story's about.

That's right, folks, a young dolphin, Duffy by name.
Because of him, golf hasn't been quite the same.
For Duffy developed a talent most keen
At home, by the shore of the 18th hole green.

He lived in a golf course's waterhole pool
And I'll say that dolphin was one golfin' fool.
By swinging his tail, like a golf club in hand,
He hit pearls, like golfballs, from off of the sand.

For since he's been but a wee duffer of three,
He'd taken golf lessons, entirely free,
And saw how to play the game "going to school,"
By watching the pro golfers play from his pool.

Duff played on a course that was wonderfully grand,
A paradise wrapped in a blanket of sand,
With coral-bound fairways and tall seaweed roughs,
Where pearls are golf balls and dolphins are duffs.

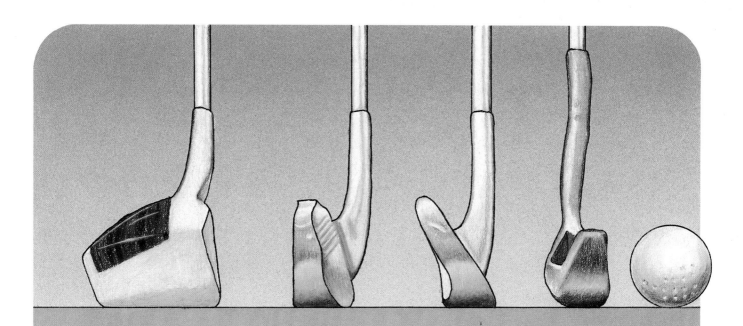

Duff took all he saw and he heard straight to heart;
That dolphin looked promising right from the start.
He watched many golfers, but copied just one,
And learned how each shot in that pro's bag was done.

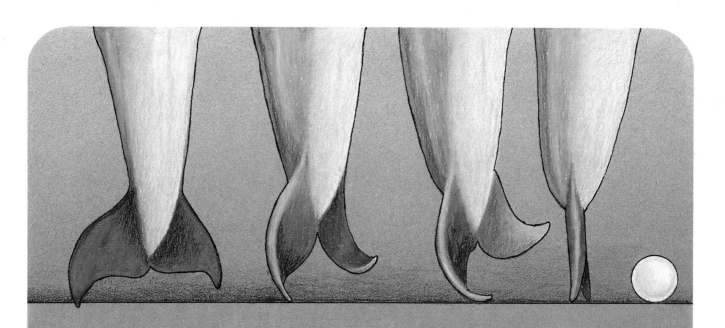

Determined, Duff worked on his golf game a lot.
By angling his tail, he could vary each shot.
Less angle for distance, more angle for height.
With practice, he mastered each angle just right.

Now putting's the trickiest part of the game,
So Duff lined his putts up with accurate aim.
He did this with help from some oysters, you see.
When ready, he'd ask them, "Please open for me."

The oysters would open their shells very wide
So Duffy could practice by putting inside.
Then all of them spit the pearls back out to Duff,
Except for one crabby and horrible huff.

And that oyster, called Selfish Shellfish by name,
Was always disrupting the wee dolphin's game.
He'd clam up Duff's putting-pearls when he could,
And would not return them, though he knew he should.

So Duffy would ask, in a most polite way,
"Please give me those pearls; I need them to play."
The shellfish would answer him back, with a gruff,
"Those pearls are mine now, so take a swim, Duff!"

But Duff kept his dream, despite Selfish, you know,
To play like the great Arnold Palmer. And so,
He studied and practiced his game, short and long,
Because, to be great, all your strokes must be strong.

Then one day some news came to Duffy's address,
By way of Sebastian Seahorse's express.
It seems Arnold Palmer was coming to play
In quite an important golf tourney that day.

In light of such news, the thrilled dolphin flipped out,
And gave a big cheer (although dolphins can't shout).
The gen'ral of golf, with his army and all,
Was going to pay Duffy's golf course a call!

So Duff swam around to the very first tee
Where Arnold his hero was scheduled to be,
In hopes of a poolside position to take
To watch all the great shots that Arnold could make.

At long last, the gen'ral did finally stride
to tee up, with caddy and clubs at his side.
And Duffy, now balancing high on his tail,
Could see Arnold's first tee shot take off and sail.

Duff followed his hero each link of the course,
For each fairway, fed by an underground source,
Had waterholes, very much like Duffy's home
Of sandy beach bottom and watery dome.

That dolphin became quite a regular sight
To Arnie, and all of his army's, delight.
With every great shot, on his tail Duffy'd stand,
And Arnold acknowledged by waving his hand.

ow Arnold, at first, found himself in a bind,
For after round one he was nine strokes behind.
But during round two he began to attack,
And by the third's end, he was just six strokes back.

He started round four with a drive of such strength
It rocketed out an incredible length,
Reminding his army, on foot and on fin,
The great Arnold Palmer was playing to win!

The cheers did resound, from the gallery's throng,
A deafening echo ten thousand times strong.
Each one of his army, from private to sarge,
Called out to their gen'ral, "C'mon Arnie, Charge!"

And charge Arnold did. He regained each lost shot
With driver, so daring, and putter, red hot.
He birdied the 12th through the 17th holes;
Too much ammunition for golf's lesser souls.

The very last hole found the tournament tied;
For victory, Arnold and two others vied.
The pressure was pounding those three golfers great.
A bad bounce . . . a wrong roll . . . could seal each one's fate.

And that final hole was a long, hard par 5,
Where sandtraps and water ate golf balls alive.
This vicious old dog leg veered off to the right,
With rough very ragged and fairway so tight.

Perched high on his tail, Duffy surveyed the scene;
The fairway was lined from the tee to the green.
The army all wondered what Arnold would do,
With breaths held, and hearts stopped, and fingers crossed, too.

He strode to the tee, while the crowd, in a trance,
All watched him line up and get set in his stance,
Then draw back his club with a powerful wince,
And let go a drive that has not been seen since.

The tee shot was super! The second just fine,
But as the third rose, a stray bird crossed its line,
And o'er Duffy's waterhole, bird and ball met;
A sight no one present will ever forget.

The ball hit the bird and dropped into the drink.
Forlorn, Duffy watched the ball and his hopes sink.
Would Arnold, now also, go down to defeat
And see his bold charge change into a retreat?

For Arnold, in order to play that doomed ball,
Would have to make magic. And folks, after all,
Though bold Arnold just might have welcomed the task,
To play golf on water's a bit much to ask.

Now everyone knew. The handwriting was clear:
The loss of his golf ball would cost Arnold dear.
He'd have to take one of golf's penalty strokes,
Which surely would cost him the tournament, folks.

A strange twist of fate, yes, a stroke of bad luck
Had run Arnold's chances for vict'ry amuck.
And Duffy, upset all the way to his core,
Just had to do something to even the score.

A masterful plan then flashed into Duff's brain.
Inspired by the need of a vict'ry to gain,
He dove through the depths of his waterhole pool,
And though he was nervous, stayed steady and cool.

He spied the ball sinking and took a brisk swing,
But couldn't quite reach it, and just missed the thing.
The ball fell too fast for Duff's golfin' tail swish,
Right into the grip of the Selfish Shellfish.

"Please give me that ball, Selfish," Duffy did plead.
"For once in your life do an unselfish deed."
"Why should I?" said Selfish. "What's in it for me?
There's no way I'll give you this golf ball for free."

At that, Duffy poised his tail, ready to swing,
As mad as a hornet, just itching to sting.
"I want that ball, Selfish, before I count five,
Or you'll be the first oyster divot alive!"

That scared Selfish Shellfish to shivers and more!
He coughed up the ball just as Duffy reached four.
Duff then quickly gripped the golf ball in his bite
And swam for the surface with all of his might.

The dolphin emerged before Arnold and all;
He spouted some water and teed up the ball.
Each one of the judges, then, had to decide
If Duffy's aid should be allowed or denied.

As all ears awaited the judges' reply,
Their verdict came down: "Play the ball at its lie!"
The air was then filled with a thunderous din
As everyone rooted for Arnold to win.

In order to win, he would have to drum up
A miracle shot, really close to the cup.
Since both of his rivals were in better spots,
The tourney was riding on this shot of shots.

And as Arnold studied that watery prop,
The silence was such, you'd have heard a tee drop.
He made his decision . . . and reached for a wedge.
Would this be the club to give Arnold the edge?

The weapon was drawn; its blade shone in Duff's view.
"I promise," said Arnold, "my club won't hurt you."
The ball bubbled up . . . the steel blade swung down
And whisked the ball off, without touching Duff's crown.

The ball was hit cleanly; the stroke felt just right.
Duff turned, and with Arnold he watched the ball's flight.
It sailed through the air, arcing into the blue
And bounced on the green toward the flag, rolling true.

That shot was the greatest of Arnold's career,
For Duff played his part without flinching from fear.
The golf ball rolled into the cup, though still damp.
The great Arnold Palmer was tournament champ!

One judge draped a medal around Arnold's neck;
Two more shook his hand, and then said with respect,
"That shot, sir, was brilliant . . . how did you do it?"
"Had to," said Arnold. "There's nothing more to it!"

His army went wild, for their gen'ral had won.
The trial, by tourney, was over and done.
As Duff watched his hero accept the award,
The wee dolphin's spirits just took off and soared.

But when the award ceremony was done,
He graciously took off the medal he'd won,
Walked over to Duffy and said with a smile,
"You're the golfin'ist dolphin I've seen in a while!"

The champ gently draped the prize o'er Duffy's snout.
Well, needless to say, Duffy really flipped out.
A feeling of pride filled him all the way through,
For wee Duffy felt like a champion, too.

Well now, it's all over. The gen'ral has gone.
His army, except one brave soldier, withdrawn.
But for that lone soldier, the mem'ries remain.
His medal would always bring those back again.